By Caid Rhymes

To Roxanne Taylor.
This story was first conceived
as I lay crippled in a hospital bed
wondering if I would ever walk again.
And there you were by my side through it all.

This book is as much a part of you as it is me.
You were there to help me to learn to walk again
And you were there editing, expanding,
and creating this first story with me.
This is our book, our story, our series.
And it is only just beginning.

Slug Girl

Chapter 1: Worthy

Darkness.

It wraps around you like a comfortable sweater.

Nothing else exists at this moment.

You are worthy, you are powerful and you are wanted.

The Universe will supply you with all you need and you will prosper.

Melle opened her eyes and smiled. "I am worthy," she

whispered to the empty room from where she sat cross-legged on the floor in her white cotton underpants. "I am powerful, and I am wanted." She repeated the mantra to herself silently, willing herself to believe it, just like the books had told her she should.

She breathed out slowly. The morning sun filtered through the threadbare curtains and illuminated the room around her. It wasn't much; the paintwork had started to peel in the corners of the off-white walls. There was a small bed with the covers roughly pulled up over the pillow, an old dresser covered in hair ties and knickknacks she had collected, a clothes rack and a small desk. The ceiling fan above made a familiar metallic click with each rotation, a sound that acted like white noise when she was trying to sleep in the chaotic house she shared with her family.

Melle closed her eyes again and inhaled, scrunching her nose up at the underlying smell of stale beer and cigarettes. It hung in the air and pushed itself into the carpet, lingering on her freshly washed laundry and clinging to her hair.

"I am worthy."

Her father, Ian, had worked as a cleaner at the local shopping mall, but ever since the virus had hit, he had been laid off. He had spent his days on the couch eating cheese puffs, drinking beer and smoking. The old cream-coloured armchair, now stained a mottled brown, was a testament to her father's apathy. Just the thought of what might have been lost to time, hidden away in the crevices between the armrest and the cushions, made her ill.

Her mother, Kellie, was once the star of the school's gymnastics team and a popular cheerleader. Shortly after graduating she had fallen pregnant and that was the end of her dreams. Or at least that was the story Kellie would start telling everyone around the sixth or seventh beer. By the time she reached double digits, her story would change to say Melle had also stolen her figure, her beauty and all the joy from her life—the only reason she kept her was for the child support payments from the government. Now Kellie was an overbearing mother whose sole purpose in life seemed to be berating Melle.

"Today," Melle mused. "Today I will tell them I am going to move out and get my own apartment." Standing in one fluid motion, she padded across to

4

the dresser and pulled on a pair of ripped blue jeans and a green tank top.

Standing at just under five foot four, she had brown wavy hair that framed a delicate face that looked like it had missed a few meals. Tired brown eyes looked at her critically from the mirror. Painfully thin, her bony arms wrapped defensively across her small chest as she pursed her lips in disapproval. At twenty years old, she resembled someone still waiting to hit puberty, when in fact puberty had hit her and left her flatter than a pancake before screeching off into the distance.

Sighing dramatically, she walked across the room to turn on her computer, nabbed the can of deodorant from beside the machine, then turned and sprayed the room liberally. The screen lit up and she tapped in her password as she took a seat. The web browser opened, automatically displaying the last viewed pages, which she ignored.

They were the wasteland that was her online existence. The testament to her failed popularity and social achievements. No one ever messaged her. Melle was three years out of school and as far as the world was concerned, she might as well have been dead.

She tabbed to the page of house listings she had recently bookmarked and smiled when she found it; John had posted the listing over a week and a half ago, offering up the two-bedroom townhouse and now his smiling face looked back at her from the screen. He was a handsome man with a strong jawline and soft lips that looked like they smiled easily. Long sandy-blond hair fell across blue eyes that promised her so many things. Melle leaned forward, stroking her finger down the side of his face before closing the gap and placing a loving kiss on it. The electricity from the screen sent light tingles across her skin, as though he was kissing her back through the hard surface. Her breath fogged up the glass and blew back over her face caressing her cheeks as she whispered, "John, show me how to be loved. Be mine."

Melle had spent a week now looking at the picture of John and thinking of all the promises that swam in those blue eyes. Now, like most mornings, the desire was starting to build. Tabbing out of the rental site, Melle opened her saved pages and clicked on a now familiar link. It was a live cam site and as she waited, her screen started to fill with a plethora of young men in various stages of undress, stroking themselves for the online viewers.

For her.

She bit her lip and cupped one small breast, twisting her nipple through the fabric as her right hand slid down to her jeans where it paused as she glanced at the closed door. The gyrations on the screen drew her attention back and she flicked open the buttons of her jeans and slid her hand beneath the fabric. Her fingertips moved in slow rhythmic circles along the edge of her underwear. She took in a long slow breath as she rocked her hips, grinding herself against the hard fabric of the chair beneath her. She arched her back and tilted her hips forward, fingers dancing lower, teasingly moving over her damp underwear as an ache built within her. Slowly, ever so slowly, she rolled her hips as her fingers brushed along her inner thigh to the edge of the damp underwear and dipped beneath it.

Tilting her head back, she watched the young men from beneath lowered lashes. Stroking themselves, up and down, hands moist with fluids. She gasped as two fingers plunged within her as she ground her hips, once, twice... Her own liquids slid across her hand as she moved in time with the men on the screen, the ache between her legs building, throbbing, cresting...

Her door slammed open and he stepped into the room. His large frame took up all the space and brought with it the smell of sour sweat and cigarettes. "Well, well, what do we have here?!" He laughed as she hurriedly flicked off the screen and scrambled to button her pants.

He walked further into the room and turned her chair towards him, stopping the motion with his knees and bent forward so that his face was close to hers, his dark pig-like eyes taking in her flushed cheeks.

He smiled slowly and reached out to grab her right wrist, bringing her wet fingers closer to him and breathed deeply, savouring the smell. Reaching forward with his other hand he cupped her face, his fingers digging into her skin as he held her roughly and slid her trapped fingers into his mouth. His wet tongue curled around her knuckles, running up and down the length of the first finger as he tasted her. His lips curved into a satisfied smile, making a wet sucking noise as he let it slide out of his mouth.

"You taste like honey," he whispered huskily and ran his tongue between her next two fingers. His foul breath washed over her and flecks of cheese puffs and saliva splattered on her cheek. "You look just like your mother." Melle tried to press herself back further into the chair but there was nowhere for her to go.

"Dad, stop," she whispered harshly and tried to push herself away just as her mother walked in.

"Oh, Ian! Stop teasing the little bitch, she's like a dog in heat." Kellie laughed and slapped Ian on the arse. "Why don't you leave her alone and take me for a ride," she said with a suggestive wink.

Taking advantage of the distraction, Melle pushed her chair back and scrambled away from her laughing father, biting back a cry of pain as strands of her hair were left caught in his hand where they had ripped free.

She ducked her head down and walked quickly across the room, bile and shame burning within her. Grabbing a change of clothes and her towel from the dresser, she choked out angrily, "Leave me alone!" pushed past her mother and ran the rest of the way to the bathroom down the hall. Their laughter echoed through the paper-thin walls behind her.

Kellie watched the little harlot run from the room and felt disgust churn within her, even as she laughed along with Ian. To think she had carried that little abomination within her! She shuddered and turned back to Ian, heat rising in her gaze as she licked her dry lips suggestively. "Someone in this house needs a good fucking and I think it should be me that does it." She strode past Ian and crawled onto her daughter's bed, bending forward as she hiked her nightdress up and wiggled her arse invitingly.

Ian looked pleased and cupped himself as he glanced around his daughter's room, then back at the woman on the bed. They really did look a lot alike. Stepping forward, he grabbed a clump of her hair roughly. Pulling her head tight to his fist, he pushed her face down into the sheets so she couldn't look back and ruin it for him. "Okay, honey, you got it. But I'm taking the back road!" He hurriedly removed his now hard dick from his grey sweatpants and buried himself between her bony arse cheeks. Kellie's response was muffled as she grunted into her daughter's pillow.

Melle turned on the shower and tried to block out the

noise of her parents fucking in her room. It was something they had been doing more increasingly recently as her father's unwanted advances had gotten more brazen. She knew her mother blamed her for his attraction and she really didn't know what to do. If only John was here, she knew he would make her father pay. "Fucking sicko," she muttered angrily, kicking her clothes into a corner and stepping into the lukewarm spray.

Melle soaped up and tried to get the water to rush over her ears to dull the sounds, as her father's groans got louder and louder. She grabbed the bottle of shampoo and washed her hair, feeling the long strands wrap around her fingers as she slowly dragged them through, paying attention to work out the few knots that could be felt. She imagined the tension leaving her body, to swirl around her toes with the suds circling the drain. Slowly the steam from the hot water engulfed the room, filling the air with the smell of the eucalyptus shampoo and for a brief moment in her mind, she was alone with not a care in the world; a small moment of peace.

A loud bang on the door, from her father's heavy fists, dragged her back into the real world. She hoped the lock would hold this time.

"For fuck's sake, Melissa, get out here," Ian yelled through the door. "Your mum has shit the bed again, and you need to clean this mess up."

Melle turned off the tap and grabbed a towel to dry herself. "Okay, Dad." She hurriedly threw on her oversized clothes and walked out of the bathroom, just in time to see her parents close their own bedroom door, giggling like teenagers.

The muffled, "Okay, you dirty girl, let daddy finish," from behind her parents' closed door, made her skin crawl and she quickly ducked into her room to see the mess they had made.

Chapter 2: Dearest mother

"I am going to have to bleach my mattress again," she sighed under her breath as she grabbed the sheets and placed them in the laundry sink. Crouching down, she opened the cupboard beneath the sink and reached for the bottle of bleach but found it empty.

"Crap. I better go get some more. The last thing I need when moving into a new place is a shit-stained mattress. What would John think?"

She filled the sink with hot water to get it soaking and ducked back into her room again. Melle quickly shoved her wallet and phone into her backpack with her Walkman and wrapped the headphones around her neck. Confident she had everything, she walked out of her room only to bump into her mother.

"Oh, look at you cleaning up the mess like a good girl. Your poor father, he used to be the man about town. All the ladies were in love with him, you know?" She looked down her nose at Melle and grimaced. "He loved you so much, you were his special girl. It's a shame you were always a little slow."

Melle felt the familiar pain in her chest as her mother's words dug at her but she tried not to let anything show, just ducked her head and nodded as she walked to the lounge room. "I am heading to the store to get more bleach and will be back soon."

"Well, you got your welfare payment this week so get us some smokes, love, and some more beer for your father. You know how he likes to watch his shows with some beer."

Melle realized this was going to eat into her moving out money and the knot that sat in the pit of her stomach clenched as she pushed the rage down inside. She wanted to scream, to lash out but instead, she sighed. She looked down at the carpet where there was a red strand of fabric and counted to ten. She briefly wondered where the red strand was from. No one owned any red clothing—it looked too clean.

Looking up and away from her mother, she calmly said, "I need it for bills, Mum." The slap took her by surprise as she felt the sting of pain.

Her mother stood nose to nose with her now, angry words coming from between clenched teeth. "I fucking raised you. I fucking paid for your clothes, food and everything else you needed. And now you don't want to chip in?"

The hate in her mother's eyes was too much and Melle quickly looked down again at the red string of fabric, furiously trying to hold back tears. "I just... I pay rent, Mum. I pay for my food now. I help." Melle winced, waiting for another hit to come, but it never did.

Instead her mother's cold voice filled the silence. "If you don't get me some smokes and a case of beer when you are out, then I will make sure you have a mark to match on the other side of your face… And THEN…" She smiled nastily at Melle. "I will let your father have his way. I bet you would LOVE that."

She drew in a sharp breath and stared back up at her mother in shock. "You wouldn't!" Melle started to say, but the cold look in her mother's eyes stopped her. She really would… "Okay, Mum, I'll get them," she said quietly as she looked away again, no longer holding back the tears.

Kellie stepped back and crossed her arms, smirking. "That's a good girl, grab us a lotto ticket as well, today's gonna be our lucky day. I just feel it."

Melle walked out of the house, closing the door behind her. As bile rose in her throat, she paused at the top of the stairs to take a few large gulps of air, but it wasn't enough. She bent over the railing and dry retched a few times as she replayed her mother's words. Surely she wouldn't actually let him? Straightening up, Melle decided to put some distance between herself and her parents.

Chapter 3: One foot in front of the other

It was a crisp morning. As Melle walked down the old wooden steps and out into the bright day, she squinted as she grew accustomed to the sun. The sky was a deep blue and not a cloud was in it. Winter was almost over and the flowering yellow wattle filled the air with a rich woody floral smell that reminded Melle of burnt caramel. It was a fresh change from the stench of her family home.

Is it even my home? she wondered, *I mean I have never felt at home there. Maybe John will be home for me.* She smiled at the thought of that. Maybe she would finally find a place to belong. She adjusted her backpack to sit more comfortably and put the headphones over her ears. Turning on the Sony Walkman, she headed to the right and walked along the footpath.

She looked down at the concrete moving beneath her feet and smiled as she playfully bounced along the pavement with a quick skip. "Step on a crack, break your mother's back." She slammed her foot down on a crack and giggled. "Step on a line. You'll break your father's spine." She joyfully sang as she brought the other foot down on the same crack. *I can only wish for that,* she mused.

Melle was suddenly interrupted by the flash of a blue and red striped tracksuit in front of her. "Step on a stick and you better suck my dick." *Michael? What was he doing here?* she thought. The boy in front of her laughed. Moving quicker than expected, he swung at her with the large stick he was carrying. It grazed her right shoulder, causing her to cry out in pain as she stumbled back out of reach. Michael pointed the stick in her direction again and looked to the side, behind the trunk of a tree nearby. "Look at what we have here, Kylie. The school retard."

Melle drew back at the mention of Kylie's name. As bad as her home life was, school life had sometimes been darker. They had once been best friends in primary school, but that all changed the year Kylie's mum had left during Christmas break. Melle had tried to reach out to her friend during those holidays but received stony silence. When school resumed, Kylie was a whole new person who pretended Melle did not exist and those first few months Melle had thought were the worst. Then what followed was years of bullying and harassment. Kylie turned all of their classmates against Melle and they followed her lead at making Melle's school life miserable well past graduation,

Kylie's smiling face appeared from behind the trunk. "O.M.G." She giggled as she drew out each letter in mock amazement. "It's Melle the Mole!" Quickly she ran over to Melle and leaned in close with feigned familiarity. "What are you doing out all alone on this sunshiny day, sweety?" The corners of her smile grew deeper in mock friendliness.

Melle shied back but Kylie grabbed her sore arm and turned back to her high school beau, a glint in her eye that made Melle feel queasy with anxiety. "Well now, Michael, you know how you were talking about a threesome this morning, maybe this is your chance?" Her lips curled and her fingernails dug in as she forced Melle to the ground between her and Michael.

Melle could feel the gravel digging into her knees, the stones grinding as she tried to stand but the stronger girl held her down. "Please don't. I just need to go to the shops, please," Melle pleaded as she looked from one to the other, then wildly around at the empty street.

"Please? Please? Please?" Michael mocked. "She is practically begging for it! But I don't know if I want to put my dick in that," he said with disgust, brushing imaginary dirt off his shoulder.

Kylie snorted in amusement, her perfect brown hair bouncing as she turned her head to the side and peered down at Melle still kneeling on the ground. "Want to play touch up the freak instead?"

"NO! Stop. You're hurting me." Kylie ignored the cries from the smaller girl as she stepped closer and dug her knee into Melle's back. Leaning forward, she grabbed a hold of Michael's collar and pulled him forward, kissing him roughly while ignoring the struggling girl caught between them. Michael grinned into the passionate kiss and hopefully asked, "Can I cum on her tits too?"

Kylie swatted his chest with her free hand and glared at him. "You couldn't find them even if you wanted to. Feel lucky I am letting you do this. Cum in her hair, at least it saves us from cleaning up and besides, that's all she deserves."

Roughly she grabbed a few strands of Melle's hair and laughed as she pretended to feel it. "Honestly, it's so dry. Her hair could use the protein. We are so selfless, helping the dregs of our society like this." Michael guffawed and licked his lips expectantly as he fumbled with the zip on his pants, hurriedly pushing them down enough to free himself.

Kylie pushed the kneeling girl's face into her boyfriend's crotch, letting Michael hold the struggling girl's head there as his dick twitched against the side of her face. Still holding Melle's arm firmly, Kylie knelt down and licked the salty trail, which was a mix of precum and tears, from Melle's cheek as she leaned in close and whispered into the smaller girl's ear, "Shit comes from shit. Your daddy fucked my mum and ruined my life. You need to understand the boundaries your shit of a father obviously doesn't know. Michael is mine!" She dug her fingers painfully into Melle's arm, eliciting another cry. Satisfied, she turned her head and captured her boyfriend's dick with her mouth, sucking it in deep before letting it fall wetly back out. "This is all you are good for."

Kylie stood back up and nodded at Michael, leaning in again to kiss him as he started to furiously jerk off. His rough hands ran down his own shaft so quickly, he knew he wasn't going to last long. Michael groaned as Kylie bit his lip and he muttered, "Here I cum, babe. All over the space cadet."

"Please no!" Melle cried out again, trying to dodge as Michael spilt himself messily across the side of her head. The hot liquid dribbled over her ear and cheek. The taste of him was at the corner of her mouth.

Kylie laughed at the sight and clapped her hands in delight. "Let me clean that off for you, babe." She leaned forward and quickly slid his semi-erect penis back into her mouth. Her tongue wrapped around the shaft eliciting a strangled gasp from her boyfriend as she pulled away again. "All clean and no more freak." She coughed and pulled a long red strand of Melle's hair out of her mouth. "Well, that is just nasty." She stood back up as Michael tucked himself back in and zipped his pants up. Kylie pushed Melle over the rest of the way and kicked the fallen girl's backpack into the street. "Now fuck off, freak."

Melle wiped her face with her sleeve and hurried to her feet, grabbing her bag from the street.

"And if you tell anyone, we will beat the shit out of you, loser!" Michael yelled as she ran off.

Chapter 4: Convenience store blues

After a few blocks, Melle stopped running. Her lungs and eyes were burning. Her hair was stuck to the side of her face and she couldn't stop crying.

Looking around to get her bearings, she darted across the road and slowly made her way up the street and rounded the corner to the empty park.

Seeing a water fountain, she went over and turned on the tap; gingerly at first, then more forcefully, she started scrubbing the semen from her hair, face and clothes. After a few minutes, she stopped crying and straightened herself up.

"No," she said forcefully. "No more crying, you are not gonna let anyone push you around anymore. You need to stand up for yourself!" Running her fingers through her messed-up hair, she hoped she looked somewhat presentable and started walking toward the store again.

Examining her headphones, she sighed with relief. They had seen better days but they looked like they survived. She plugged them back into the Walkman and slipped them on again as she blasted music to drown out the negative thoughts in her head. She had become used to being called a loser, from as early on as she could remember she had been bullied. Maybe it was because she was smaller than the other kids, or from a poor family. Or maybe because she was a dreamer. In the quiet moments, of which there were not many, that is what she would tell herself.

She had always wondered what had caused her best

friend to suddenly hate her so much. Why she insisted on calling her 'Melle the Mole' and made other kids do it as well. It wasn't until her last year of high school that she had overheard her parents fighting and her mother had brought it up, when everything had made sense. It wasn't fair but life rarely is. She had tried to talk to Kylie about their parents once but it had just made the bullying worse. Melle had kept her head down for the rest of high school and had hoped life beyond would get better.

But it wasn't. It was fucked.

But John would change that.

It was a small convenience store in the heart of her suburb. The building looked like it was made from solid cement and every window and door had been covered in bars. The outer walls were layered with years of built-up dirt, peeling yellowed paint, and old community notices of people selling or buying. There were two double doors at the front behind a twin pair of damaged cement bollards and security cameras sprouted from walls covered with angry red signs that warned away prospective shoplifters. Melle wondered if other neighborhoods had so much security for small local stores.

Pulling the aged door open, Melle darted inside as the bell above announced her entry. Letting her eyes adjust to the fluorescent lighting, Melle felt her heart sing as she saw Jackson sitting behind the counter. He was a couple of years older than her, but Melle remembered him well from high school as he had always been hanging around Kylie back then.

Jackson looked up from his phone and a wide grin came across his face. "Melle the Mole," he repeated a few times, drawing out the vowels. "It's been a few years. Do you live around here, freak?"

"I'm not a freak. I am worthy," she replied defensively and immediately regretted it.

"You are worthy?" He laughed and stood to lean over the counter to gesture towards the door. "What kind of bullshit response is that? Get the fuck out of here, loser."

Melles eyes widened and panic made her chest hurt as she cried out, "But I need to buy some stuff!"

Jackson leaned back again and laughed derisively. "Do I look like I care? While my old man is away this is my store and I have standards." Puffing his chest up with importance, he made a shooing motion towards the door. "Go to the supermarket. They will serve anyone, even freaks like you."

Melle started to protest but Jackson cracked his knuckles in warning. Getting the message, she turned and left the store.

The supermarket was a good hour or more walk away. Turning left out of the store, Melle walked along the pavement a few metres and turned to lean her back against the yellowed wall. Melle looked down at her left foot, the hole in her shoe had opened up again. She really needed to buy new shoes, but that had to wait until she had moved out. Until then, any spare cash she had would go towards saving up for a place of her own. *A place with John,* she thought.

He had his own car and they would drive into the main city and shop at the big supermarkets once a week. They would pool their resources together and instead of the Black and Gold cheap brands she normally bought, they would get real brands with logos and everything. She pulled her backpack off her shoulder, placed it on the ground in front of her and rummaged inside. She knew she had a cheap roll of duct tape for emergency clothing and shoe repair she had gotten from Silly Sallies, a dollar store just off the highway near her house.

Pulling it from her bag, she started picking at the end of the roll, trying to lift it with her chewed nails. Finally she teased the corner up and pulled a section clear to start wrapping her shoe. The last round of tape had lasted twenty-three days since she had wrapped the hole that today's adventures had reopened. *Adventures,* she thought bitterly—*more like nightmares.*

She wrapped a couple more layers around the top of the shoe and surveyed her work. That should do for another few weeks. She placed the duct tape back into her bag and started walking in the direction of the supermarket.

Running her fingers along the rough brickwork, she sighed. It would take more than a couple of hours to walk there and back home again. There would not be enough time to clean and dry the mattress. Her parents were going to be furious at her for taking so long to get them their smokes and drinks, something they surely would take out on her.

The wall ended and curved off to the left into the

alleyway that ran along the back of Jackson's store. As she crossed the shadowed entryway a loud noise from above caught her attention. Looking up Melle saw a bright green light in the sky heading right for her.

Chapter 5: Slug from outer space!

Melle threw herself to the ground and a loud crash came from behind her as the green light hit the ground. Chipped cement and asphalt sprayed painfully across her back and sides as she curled up to protect her face. After what seemed like an age, it stopped and she carefully pulled herself up, wiping blood and dust from various scratches on her arms.

Turning around, Melle looked to see what happened to the store behind her but the building was in one piece with no sign of damage.

Confused for a moment, Melle blinked and wiped the dust from her face. The Alleyway! That had to be where it landed. If it was a meteor, then she could sell it online. *Surely that would sell for a small fortune,* she thought. With the money she would make she would be able to move out and be with John. *Finally, the Universe is supplying me with what I need.* She peered into the shadows and looked for an impact site. Surely a meteor landing would make a crater but where is it?

With hurried steps she made her way into the alley, dodging debris and trash. It was just wide enough for a single car to fit down it - as long as you didn't want to open your doors. Old metal drum barrels were grouped along the walls and a large dumpster sat midway down at an odd angle, its pitted surface graffitied with the familiar *T3N31* slogan of the local teenage rebels.

She shook her head to chase the wandering thoughts away and focused on what she was doing. Her semi-damp hair fell across her eyes and she tucked it behind her ear. Her fingers made their way to her mouth and she nervously started to chew on them as she picked her way along the alley.

As Melle approached the dumpster, she could see a slimy viscous liquid on the ground forming a splatter shape which appeared to trail off and around the far corner of the bin into the shadows behind. It looked like someone had soaked a tennis ball in green tinged KY Jelly and slammed it on the ground.

Kneeling down to take a closer look, Melle winced as she felt the scrapes on her knees touch the ground and open up again with sharp little stings. She stretched her hand out to touch the slime but paused midway as a stray thought crossed her mind. *It could be poisonous or even toxic.*

Biting her lip, she made up her mind and leaned down to drag two fingers through the liquid. Sparks arced along her hand and into her body as an electric current ran through her, knocking her backwards as darkness enveloped her.

Hello, a deep voice resonated inside Melle's head.

Groaning Melle rolled onto her side and groggily sat up. "Who is there?" she called to the empty alleyway.

I am, replied the voice.

"Who are you, where are you?" She looked around and touched her head, wondering if she had bumped it as the voice sounded like it came from within her. "Are you real?"

Of course Glurmo is real! the voice resonated in her head much louder now and tinged with desperation. *The slime made contact possible, but we need more contact, more connection, more touch for our survival.*

Melle carefully stood and looked back at the slime trail leading to behind the dumpster. Automatically she started to take a few quick steps towards it but caught herself, her mind brimming with possibilities. But the main one stuck there in front of her mind, like a song stuck in her head. *This was… is the meteor.* She took another step closer to the dumpster. *But that would mean…*

Yes, yes - I am not of this Earth. The voice agreed with her unspoken thought. *And I need you in order to survive, I am going to come out now,* it warned.

Melle's mouth formed an O of surprise as two small eyestalks peered cautiously around the corner. Shock was quickly replaced by curiosity and Melle knelt down, barely even noticing the pain in her knees or the slime beneath them as she looked into the bright purple, gelatinous eyes. Slowly as she waited, a slim slug-like body the size of a small spaniel slid around the corner of the dumpster. It was the colour of dark-green jade and was covered in the same slime that she had found on the ground. It came to a stop directly in front of her, the eyestalks almost level with her own eyes. If she reached forward she would be able to run her fingers through the slime that she could see coated its body.

It is, as you would say, a sort of slime. It also has telepathic and psychokinetic properties per se, the voice answered the question that had been rolling across the front of her mind. *That and other things.* The slug raised itself up a little and the eyestalks focussed directly on her. *I am a Glurmo of the Armislima Sexus, and I come in peaceful, albeit tragic circumstances.*

Melle took a deep breath and let it out slowly as a million questions raced across her mind. "So you're an explorer, a traveler from space, an ALIEN?" Melle questioned with excitement.

No, Glurmo's voice said sadly. *I am no explorer. I am an outcast banished here to this rock.* Glurmo lowered its eyestalks in a universal gesture of shame. *I have been abandoned here to die. Unless I find a host.*

"A host?" Melle asked, suddenly feeling flushed. "What do you mean?"

Glurmo slid a little closer, the slime from its body mingling on the ground with the blood from her cut knees. *My species is unique in the galaxy. Once we mature, we must bond with another life form in order to survive.* Glurmo's voice rolled through Melle until she thought she could almost feel the words running along her skin.

We give them unique abilities and they provide us with the energy we require. As its words vibrated in her head, Melle felt a warmth travel down to her pussy and she could feel herself moisten with each syllable it spoke.

Yes, yes, Glurmo purred into her mind. *You feel my true power, my true purpose. I can see your memories, your shame, and your desires. You want revenge and even deeper, you want to be wanted, taken and filled.* Liquid warmth pooled between her legs and her breathing came out in small gasps as electricity sparked along every nerve ending.

You want to be filled and fulfilled. Glurmo's words rolled over her and Melle leaned backwards onto the cement, leaning on one elbow as she lazily looked at the creature from between her spread legs, biting the nails on her free hand nervously. "You, you can do this?" She shifted and fought the sudden urge to finger herself in front of the slug.

Glurmo slid closer, allowing slime to drip down into her exposed panties and she gasped as a cool breeze let her know her underwear was now gone. Glurmo seductively whispered from within, *I can do this and more if you bond with me, let me fill you and empower you.*

Unable to hold back, Melle reached down and ran

her hands along Glurmo's slick body before pulling her hand back and sliding two fingers along the lips of her pussy. She slowly teased her clit as the slime sent heat-filled tingles through her core. She closed her eyes and the decision made, she pulled her hand free as she whispered, "Join with me."

As you wish.

Glurmo slowly slid up and over her pussy; she could feel a delightful, lubricated suction as it did so. A fiery tingle ran from her head to her toes as the slug slowly rolled across her clit, each small movement setting fire to her nerves. Her body was on fire, it was too much.

She bit back a cry and forced herself to look down at Glurmo. "Please," she whispered. Glurmo thrust deep inside her and she came. Her body pulsated around the writhing slug and a faint glow enveloped them both as the union was complete. Her legs shuddered and she fell back, breathless onto the pavement. "Wow. Just wow," she said as she looked up at the blue sky above and slowly stroked Glurmo's slick skin.

Chapter 6: Clean up on aisle three...

Melle sat up and brushed the dirt from her scraped knees, surprised not to find the grazes that had been there previously. She had never felt like this before. She giggled and wondered if this was what drunk with power meant. She felt strong, really strong.

Absently she reached between her legs and stroked

the slug that stayed buried partly within her. "Is this your doing Glurmo? I feel so different, and my knees are healed."

It is part of the bond that has formed between us. Just as you aid to sustain me, I aid to sustain you. We are as one now, Glurmo murmured sleepily in her mind, its voice resonating with a warmth deep within her that brought a flush to her skin. *We are worthy, We are powerful and We are wanted,* it said softly.

"Woah," Melle closed her eyes and tried to hold back the tears as she fought down the emotions that wanted to overwhelm her. Roughly she whispered, "The Universe will supply us with all we need and we will prosper." She was not alone anymore. Glurmo was with her and it needed her.

With renewed purpose Melle stood and finished brushing herself down and straightened her clothing. "You know what, we ain't walking two fucking hours to the shops, Glurmo." She walked to the entry of the alley and turned right, heading back towards the store. "Jackson is going to give us what we need."

Yes, he will. Glurmo pulsed inside her and she felt more alive than ever before. She reached the store and kicked the door open.

"What the fuck!" Jackson yelled as Melle stepped through the broken doorway. "I told you not to come in here, you fucking loser, and now look what you've done!"

Melle looked from the wrecked doorway and back to Jackson as equal parts excitement and pleasure ran through her. "Me? Obviously this is a Work Health and Safety issue, you should probably have looked at the rusted hinges years ago."

"That's it," he snarled and reached under the counter, pulling the cricket bat free that his father had in case of emergency. "Fuck this and fuck you, you broke-arsed bitch. You are going to pay for that door one way or another." He strode angrily around the counter brandishing the cricket bat.

Melle started to step back as Jackson came towards her, putting her hands up to ward off the bat as he swung it at her head - then she felt it. A warm rush to her groin and pleasure exploded between her thighs as Glurmo seemed to spread upwards and out. Her clothing disintegrated as the slug grew, and reshaped itself, flowing down her legs, up across her chest and around her back creating a throbbing exoskeleton with a hard shell.

Jackson's eyes widened in shock as much as her own did and neither were prepared for the tentacles that burst from the armor to reach forward and snatch the bat from him, stopping its forward momentum. Jackson stumbled backwards as he looked at her in fear. "I knew you were a freak."

Anger rolled through Melle in hot waves and the tentacles responded by snapping the bat in half and lurching forward menacingly at Jackson. He stood frozen with fear as they dropped the broken bat and slowly started curling around the arm that had brandished it. "What. What are you doing? This is… Just no." He tried pulling his arm free but it wouldn't budge.

A slow smile spread across Melle's face. She felt powerful, she was powerful. "I want a bottle of bleach, some smokes, and some beer," she said as Jackson refocussed on her and sneered. "No fucking way, we don't serve freaks like you, get the fuck out!"

"Maybe you didn't hear me?" she replied.

Jackson cried out in pain as spikes slowly grew along the sides of the tentacle wrapped around his arm. "What the fuck?" he swore, as they started to puncture his arm. "Fuck, fuck, fuck. Sure, sure. Whatever you want, just take it," Jackson cried, his other hand grasping at the tentacle as it wrapped itself tighter. "What are these things? What are you? Oh gods, please stop, it hurts."

"These things?" Melle responded. "They're mine." Another tentacle darted forward and slashed across Jackson's left cheek, his skin shredding as the warm liquid flowed from the wound. He screamed and tried to run, but the tentacles had him steadfast; he struggled to escape but had nowhere to go.

Melle felt Glurmo pulse from deep inside her, a feeling of pure ecstasy rolling across her senses in time with Jackson's jerky movements. Like a fly caught in her web. *Show him, Melle. Show him your new power,* Glurmo's voice slid along her insides, encouraging her, pushing her, reminding her.

"Do you remember all those times in high school you teased me, pushed me and hurt me?" More tentacles snapped forward and caught his free arm and then his legs. Slowly Jackson rose into the air, suspended, facing her as blood and snot ran down his face. "It's time you pay for that, Jackson."

Melle threw her head back in ecstasy as more tentacles erupted from her chest and sides, shooting forward to whip across Jackson's suspended body. Tearing and shredding. Every movement brought her closer to fulfillment. Biting her lip, she faced him as the spikes caught on him ripping chunks of flesh, hair, clothing and goop with each lash.

"It wasn't me, it was the others," he cried desperately as his voice cracked. "Please stop," he whimpered as specks of blood bubbled from between his lips. The spiked tentacles gouged deep into exposed bones and he fell silent. Blood splattered across Melle's limbs and the deep pulsing grew stronger as the tentacles pounded relentlessly against his skull. With a crack it opened and the sludge inside spilled out. There was a wet thud as the tentacles let go and dropped Jackson's lifeless corpse to the floor.

The spikes slowly retracted and reformed into small slits that opened along the length of the tentacles and they began to gorge on the remains of Jackson, slowly sucking his life blood from the floor. The liquid vibrating up along the length of the tentacles pushed

Melle over the edge as fire erupted along her nerve endings and pleasure rolled through her in fiery waves of delight. Slowly the tentacles lowered her to the floor to writhe amongst the blood and viscera..

Slowly Melle opened her eyes. She could feel Glurmo humming along her clit, satisfied and pleased with itself. "What was that, Glurmo?" She felt lighter than she had in a long time. Something had changed and her world would never be the same again. "Is it always like this?" she asked, her hand absently stroking the slug between her legs. She could feel it moving within her, tentacles probing her depths, bringing her small shocks of pleasure.

Yes, she could hear Glurmo reply. *It will always be like this, all I need is your pleasure and I will help you reach that climax in any way that brings you satisfaction. Through mutual pleasure we will grow strong and more powers will become available. The skin that flows over you now is just the start, and the bio-limbs will help reshape your world.* She shuddered and smiled as the early afternoon sun sent sunbeams to dance along the nearby wall.

"Oh Shit!" she cried and scrambled to her feet. "I

need to get Mum's smokes." She quickly ran behind the counter, looked at the wall of cigarettes and grabbed a couple of packets. She reached for her purse but realised that beyond the exoskeleton, now covering most of her body like a greenish second skin, she had nothing else on her.

Take the money, take all the money, Glurmo said, then she giggled and opened the cash register. There was a collection of notes, roughly a few hundred. "I guess we will have enough to move out now." She reached forward but a tentacle beat her to it and absorbed the money into itself.

You will want for nothing. If you need it, we will take it from now on, the slug said, filling her with warm confidence. *Nothing can stop us, Melle.* She moved quickly through the aisles grabbing the bleach and the beers.

Ducking back to the counter, she picked up a lighter and took one last look around the store. "Okay, let's go home. I need to have a talk with my parents."

Chapter 7: Give it to me Mickey!

Melle marvelled at her day as she walked back across the abandoned park towards her usual neighbourhood. Here she was walking in a pair of dead man's shoes, wearing a pink beanie and stolen sunnies from the corner store she had just set fire to and life was good. She had started out alone and now she would never be that again. Glurmo pulsed within her in a very happy manner that made her misstep as her pussy tightened appreciatively.

In the distance Melle could hear a familiar nasal laugh that she remembered from that morning. Hate filled her as she put the beers and bleach down. "Michael…"

Michael and three others were loitering on the park benches when he noticed Melle walking across the park in their direction. "There she is, peeps. The freak herself. Hey, Melle, thirsty for some more?" He grabbed his crotch suggestively. "Loving the spandex. I have mates who wouldn't mind saying hello!"

The group got up and started catcalling as they walked towards her. Michael at the front, followed by a large oafish boy called Jason, a short thin guy and his girlfriend. Melle knew them all from her school days. They had always joined in on her attacks but never been so bold to do it in public. What exactly had Michael told them?

As power filled her, Melle found herself walking confidently up to stand in front of Michael. *This is the one, then? The one who humiliated you earlier?*

"Yes," Melle replied as she looked up into Michael's shocked face.

"You are ready for round two?" He looked nervously between Melle and his mates who responded with grins and more catcalls. "Alright, maybe we can have a bit more fun this time, but no one tells Kylie."

Sarah, a redhead with a smattering of freckles across her cheeks, stepped forward and grabbed Melle's hands in mock support. "I am gonna shove so many things inside your ass as the others fuck you." They all laughed and Melle just smiled sweetly at them.

"What the fuck is wrong with you?" Michael pulled Sarah back as he glared at Melle. "Ain't you afraid?"

"Afraid? No. No, I am so ready for this Michael, so ready," she replied serenely.

Melle took a step back and spread her arms out, her fingers splayed in supplication. She shuddered as the first orgasm from the tentacles sliding out of her body fluttered through her. From her back, tentacles rose and hovered over her shoulders menacingly. "Oh, God, yes," she moaned and focused on

Michael. "I am sure you have seen enough porn to know where this is going."

Jason, the large oafish boy who had been watching silently the whole time—with his hands in his pockets —turned to run. The tentacles lashed out, grabbed him by the ankles and lifted him into the air above the shocked group. Melle laughed and another tentacle snaked out and wrapped around his head, covering his mouth and nostrils. It began squeezing. The boy clawed at the slime-covered appendage but it didn't budge. He reached out desperately to his friends but they stumbled back beyond his reach. Jason's eyes started to bulge and blood flowed down his tear-stained cheeks. His face turned a purplish-red colour and bubbles frothed in his eyes as vessels began to burst from the pressure.

Melle threw her head back as Glurmo pulsed approvingly within her and she shuddered. "Oh, my God, I'm cumming." She arched her back and gasped as she reached her climax. In an instant, Jason's head was crushed like a ripe melon and blood splattered over his friends. More tentacles sprouted from the bio-armour on her back and she turned and smiled seductively at Michael. "Don't worry, sweetie, I will be slow with you. I am a freak like that."

Tentacles shot towards the group, releasing them from the frozen shock that had held them and they turned to flee as they screamed in terror. Michael slipped in something that used to be attached to Jason and fell hard to the ground. A tentacle shot past him and attempted to latch onto Dan, who pushed his girlfriend into its path, even as another wrapped around his chest, binding his arms to his side. Michael scooted backwards but another tentacle was already curled around his foot.

Melle stepped forward and ran her fingers along the slick surface that now encircled Sarah's right wrist. The redhead cried and cursed as she tried to pull her arm free of the vice-like grip. Melle directed another tentacle to curl around the girl's left leg, locking her in place as the appendage slowly made its way to the bottom of her skirt.

Leaning forward, Melle grabbed a handful of Sarah's hair and pulled her head to the side, forcing the trapped girl to look at her as the tentacle moved higher up her leg. "What was that you were saying about shoving stuff up my arse?" Sarah's eyes widened, her mouth falling open in surprise as the tentacle ran itself around the shocked woman's suddenly clenched arsehole.

"Brace yourself, honey, I am going in." Sarah let out a howl as the tentacle roughly thrust into her ass and pushed its way upwards. She coughed up blood and gurgled apologies as the tentacle started tearing at her insides as it mercilessly moved upwards and thrust itself out from between her lips in a blood-filled gush, splitting the now limp body apart.

Melle smiled and turned back to Dan, who was struggling and trying to bite the appendages that had him wrapped up like a human piñata. "No biting!" she chided and reached out to pat the tentacle that had just forced its way through Sarah. It leaned into her touch like an adoring puppy and the end slowly opened like a flower, revealing a gaping maw of razor teeth. "That's our job!"

The tentacle snapped forward, tearing through his cheap chinos and wriggling inside. "No. No no, please," he screamed as the probing limb found his penis and clamped down.

"I wonder how many tugs to get him off?" Melle

laughed and wrenched the tentacle back and forth with her mind. Much too soon it ripped free, the blood from the torn penis spraying all over Dan's face as he passed out. Melle giggled and called out, "Bukakae!" as she slammed the tentacle into his mouth, lodging his shredded manhood down his throat to suffocate him.

"Glurmo, this connection, this power. I am so fucking getting off on all of this," she said as the tentacles writhed around her, pulsing in time with her latest climax.

This power is ours to share for eternity, those who treated us like trash will pay for their sins in blood and so much more, the creature spoke into her mind.

"Speaking of sins," she turned to Michael. "Hello, lover."

The tentacle currently wrapped around the struggling form released him and he fell to the ground amongst the blood and viscera. Scrambling to his feet, Michael tried to run but the tentacles turned him back to face Melle.

"You can't do this," he cried angrily as he faced her. "You're a fucking freak, a loser."

"I can and I will. You are nothing and soon you will be no one." She smiled at him and reached out with the tentacles to encircle each of his limbs, once more entrapping him. They forced him to the ground to lay spread-eagle on his back as she stood next to him.

Glurmo pulses, thrusting itself encouragingly within her. *This is the boy that violated you, yes?* the creature asks.

"He is," Melle responded as she looked at the struggling form.

Then let us devour him slowly and drain his energy for ourselves.

"That sounds delicious," said Melle.

Michael threw his head around frantically looking around at whoever Melle was talking to. "Who the fuck are you talking to, you crazy bitch?"

Melle slowly stepped over him, one leg on either side of his waist and ran her hand down the exoskeleton of her belly to between her legs as tentacles slid out from within her.

"What the fuck!" exclaimed Michael. "You fucking freak!" The tentacles pulled Michael's limbs tighter and he screamed in pain.

"Now, now, name calling will get you nowhere, Mikey. I can call you Mikey, can't I?" The tentacles slowly nipped at his clothing and tore through his jeans

"Fuck you, you crazy cunt!" he screamed as another tentacle snapped out and wrapped itself around his head, muffling his screams but leaving him to stare out at her in terror.

"Hush, babe," Melle crooned intimately. "You said you wanted to cum inside me, right?" The slick arms slowly made their way up his boxer legs and tugged the material from his body, exposing his dick.

"Hmmm, not that excited I see. Well I mean it is cold out, right?" Melle slowly started rubbing between her legs and Glurmo extended itself out from within her, dangling between her legs like green coloured misshapen testes.

Michael's muffled screams sent pleasure through

them both as Glurmo opened an unusually large mouth, revealing circular teeth that resembled those of a lamprey. Slime dripped from within as it lowered itself down and clamped around Michael's flaccid dick.

Melle marvelled as Michael thrashed even harder, while the noises he was making somehow intensified. Her eyes rolled back and the tentacles held her up as wave after wave of pleasure rolled over her as the slug started to suck. Power filled her with each pulse as Glurmo not only sucked the flesh, blood and goop out from Michael but also his essence.

His skin started to lose its elasticity and firmness and two tentacles unfolded their deadly mouths and began lashing and stripping off the loose flesh and devouring it as well. There was a faint glow as the creature feasted on Michael, his eyes now grey and lifeless, his last breath gone.

Melle was lost on a wave of power as Glurmo pulsed and moved along her pussy as it feasted, sharing everything with her. Slowly she opened her eyes as the pleasure receded and looked down at the crushed skeletal remains that were once Michael.

"You really eat a lot for such a little guy."

The bio-suit takes considerable energy to sustain its powers. Much biomatter is needed for the suit just as sexual energy is needed to sustain me, replied Glurmo as the tentacles pulsed pleasantly and retracted back into the bio-suit.

Melle considered its words for a moment as she crouched down and felt through the remains of Michael's jeans. "Well I do have a lot of bullies and perverts to sort out, so I guess we will be fine." Pulling out a brown wallet, she frowned down at the smiling boy on the driver's license.

I can sense your thoughts, I know you are troubled. Just ask me.

Melle tossed the wallet and walked over to Sarah's corpse and retrieved her shirt and skirt. The tentacles had done a good job of sucking the moisture out of the bloodied clothing, leaving it stained but wearable. Slowly pulling them on, she took a deep breath and centered her thoughts as she considered her questions. "Why are you here? I mean, I know how, but why did they dump you here? Why did you pick me? How long are we going to do this?"

They were ignorant and jealous of my power! came the harsh response and Melle could feel the hatred in its voice. *They banished me here where they thought I would not find a worthy host. But I found you. Your loneliness drew me to you like a beacon. I knew you needed me as much as I needed you.*

"Lonely? Me?" Melle scoffed. "I'm not lonely, I have John and my family."

The pleasure slowly receded and Melle could feel Glurmo looking intently at her from within her own mind.

Your family deserves to die and John doesn't know you exist. Don't you remember?

You are worthy, you are powerful and you are wanted.

The Universe will supply you with all you need and you will prosper.

I heard you and I came.

You are worthy and the Universe sent me to you.

It sent us to each other.

Melle could feel her eyes burning as she tried to hold back the tears, the weight of Glurmo's words rolling through her. John had been the only thing keeping her together these last few months but she knew Glurmo's words to be true. She had never met John and he had never responded to any of her emails. Melle leaned into the tentacles that had softly slipped out to embrace her as she cried out her fears.

Chapter 8: Kill the bitch!

The walk back to her house was surprisingly quick as a new purpose guided her steps. She was going to show her parents she was no wallflower and she was going to take control back. After they dealt with her parents they would be free to live their lives any way they wanted. They could get a van and travel across the country, cleaning up the streets like fucking Batman! Nothing could stop them while they had each other.

Melle was so caught up in her thoughts that she didn't notice Kylie standing by the corner fence of her parents' house until she almost walked into her.

"Hey, freak," came Kylie's voice, sending a jolt of fear through Melle who stumbled to a stop in front of the blonde.

Glurmo flexed and pulsed along her nerves and new power rushed through her as she straightened her back and looked Kylie in the eye. "Hey, cunt, ready for some action?" Melle pulled back her fist and struck Kylie in the face. Or she would have if the girl hadn't moved faster than expected.

Kylie grabbed Melle's wrist and twisted, using the momentum to spin her around and tossed the smaller girl into the street. "Stay in the gutter where you belong." Kylie laughed and pretended to check her nails for chips.

Melle ignored the pain from the rescraped palms and knees as she stood and faced her high school bully. Slowly, she let the armour slide over her skin, filling her with the power to match the confidence she had initially struck with. "I'm not going to be such an easy target anymore."

Kylie's eyes widened in surprise as the armour started to cover Melle, the tentacles slid out and reared back, ready to strike her down. Cowering, Kylie raised her hands to cover her face in fear but the action was interrupted by her sudden giggle as she peeked out from behind her upheld hands. "I'm sorry, I know you are trying to scare me but I just can't keep a straight fucking face." She looked scathingly down her nose at Melle. "I mean, I knew you were a freak, but to team up with Glurmo? What loser convention did you two hook up at?"

The tentacles faltered as uncertainty slipped into Melle's thoughts. "How do you know that name?"

Kylie responded with a quick punch to Melle's face, rocking the smaller girl's head back and filling her mouth with the coppery taste of blood. "How?" She peeled her jacket off to reveal a matching exo-suit. "Glurmo's superior told me all about the loser they were sent here to find." Tentacles grew from the suit, pulsing rhythmically in the afternoon sun as it glinted off their golden surface.

Oh, no, Glurmo thought. *She is bonded with Brillip.*

"Fuck," Melle spat the blood on the ground to her left.

"Of course, you have a slug too," Melle said.

"Slug?" Kylie scoffed as she crossed her arms and ran her fingers along the slick surface, coating them. "Only you would call an alien life form by something so juvenile." The tentacles from Kylie's armour lashed out and struck at Melle, but Glurmo reacted and blocked them, the spines from the tentacles ripping at Glurmo's skin, causing both Glurmo and Melle to cry out as pain lanced through them.

From the base of Kylie's neck two eyestalks popped out and looked at Melle around either side of the blonde's head. "They want you to know it's nothing personal. Just a prank that went too far. They meant to dump Glurmo with the trash on our planet. They were happy to lose the failure but decided it was too risky to leave it alive." A cruel smile twisted Kylie's face "You getting in the way is a bonus for me."

Golden tentacles snapped out and whipped towards Melle but were interrupted as Glurmo wrapped a tentacle around Kylie's foot, pulling it out from under her. The golden tentacles shot back to wrap protectively around her at the last minute as Kylie hit the ground with a thud.

"You bitch!" she snarled at Melle from the ground. "You think you and your loser friend are gonna stop us?" The golden tentacles raised her up like a spider carrying a rag doll and placed her back on her feet. She ran at Melle screaming incoherently.

The two girls slammed together, the impact sending them tumbling into the street, where the green and golden tentacles fought for dominance as the two humans were locked in battle. Melle managed to grab Kylie by the hair and pull sharply, fistfuls of blonde strands fell to the ground. Her victory was short lived as tentacles—faster than Glurmo's, stronger than Glurmo's—subdued the green ones and started ripping furiously at Melles clothes, tearing her exposed flesh beyond the boundaries of the exosuit.

Kylie turned the struggling girl away from her and looked at Melles bare back in confusion.

The slug on Kylie's neck, looked on silently, its tentacles waving in front of her questioningly. Slowly they turned the bound girl around and peeled the last vestiges of the torn skirt from her body. Kylie's eyes widened as she looked at the pulsing slug wrapped across Melles groin. "You fucking freak!" She pushed

Melle away from her in disgust, sending the smaller girl tumbling to the ground in front of her.

Kylie cocked her head to the side, listening as the golden slug spoke to her silently. "Brillip says what you two have done is an abomination, you can never be separated with a connection like this."

"Glurmo was shunned for failing to connect with a host. If they had known this was the only way they would succeed… It is forbidden, and the penalty is death. Brillip wishes they had known sooner so you could have been spared." She smiled and cracked her knuckles. "But not me, this is fucking gross and I'm gonna crush your skull with my boots, bitch." She kicked at Melle, her foot connecting with her face and Melle felt one of her teeth come loose. The green tentacles pulled back and the exo-suit flowed out to cover Melle in a protective shield. Kylie screamed in frustration as her fists and the golden tentacles beat down on the shiny surface.

Glurmo's quiet voice spoke to Melle, *I'm sorry. I can't beat them, they always win. Always, there is pain.*

"No!" Melle refused. "We have the power! We are meant to make them all pay, you said the Universe sent you to me!"

The Golden tentacles cracked Melle's shield and ripped across her exposed shoulder and she screamed in pain trying to twist away. Kylie's laughing face filled the opening as the golden tentacles grabbed hold of the edges and slowly pulled them apart until at last the exo-suit cracked and Glurmo's pain-filled cry filled Melle's mind.

Aaahhhhhh

Blood flecks splattered over Kylie's manic face as the spiked tentacles ripped across Melle's exposed ribs and breasts and she laughed, throwing a fist into Melle's face for good measure. Melle's ribs cracked from the ferocious onslaught and she fell to the ground, temporarily released from the hold of the tentacles. She tucked her legs close to her chest and hugged herself, trying to protect herself from the pain.

Kylie started kicking the girl on the ground. "You thought you were special. You thought you had found an alien friend and were gonna be the big bad girl on the block. Well, you are not special and you never will be."

As Kylie lashed out, Melle thought *how can she be so strong, how can Kylie do this?*

Emotions, Glurmo responded. *Anger is what powers Brillip and their host's connection. Sometimes it is jealousy or joy, sadness or even fear. A connection like ours is forbidden and I am sorry.*

"But why? Why is it forbidden?"

It links us too close, confusing the connection and what powers it. It makes it unpredictable, makes us unpredictable.

"Maybe that is what we need right now, Glurmo," Melle said, a plan forming. "Take me. Take all of me. Not just the sad girl who wanted to be loved, take my anger, my rage, my fear. Take my hopes, my desires and my dreams. We are worthy. We are Powerful".

And You are Wanted, Glurmo finished for them both.

Kylie fell back as a bright glow surrounded the bleeding girl on the ground, briefly blinding her. As she blinked the spots out of her eyes and stepped forward to land another kick, Melle leapt up and knocked the breath out of her with a solid swing to her torso.

Caught off guard, Kylie folded forward and threw up, vomit spraying across her shoes. Angrily she glared at Melle. "You bitch, you're going to pay for that." The golden tentacles shot forward to hit Melle, but this time Glurmo stopped one and ripped it from Kylie's suit causing the blonde to shriek in pain as agony ripped through her connection with Brillip. "You can't do this. We are better."

Melle spat blood at Kylie and laughed. "I've been beaten and abused for as long as I can remember. And I have learned one thing recently," Melle said and threw a punch, hitting Kylie in the nose. It broke and blood oozed from her nostrils. The golden tentacles went limp as a disorientated Kylie was overtaken by fear. "I can take a beating, and you guys cannot."

Melle and Glurmo sent the green tentacles forward to wrap around Kylie's head, reaching behind to find the golden slug they knew would be attached to their rival's neck. The mouths on the questing tentacles opened and ripped into the slug mercilessly. "I am no longer being ridiculed, I am taking my life back today," Melle forcefully stated with conviction as

Glurmo's armour extended over her whole body. The tentacles, now done with Brillip, latched onto either side of Kylie's face, lifting her up into the air to Melle's eye level. She leaned in closer to the crying blonde. "I am the one with the power now, you fucking cunt." With those final words, she ripped Kylie's screaming face apart.

The tentacles shredded Kylie's limp body and drained the life essence from her as Melle flopped down on the grass nearby, emotionally and physically exhausted. Sitting quietly for a few minutes Melle recalled what Kylie had said, "You were an outcast like me then?"

Yes, Glurmo replied. *I was a laughingstock amongst my people, a failure for never finding a connection.*

"Well, now we are free from ridicule, and can create a new future for us both."

I would like that indeed, Glurmo responded after a moment.

"But first, I need to see my parents." Melle stood and collected the remains of her clothes, shaking off the majority of the fluids and other things she did not want to focus on. She walked over to Kylie's shrivelled body. Near her was a handbag the dead girl had dropped. Melle rummaged through it and found a makeup mirror. Flipping it open, she took stock of the damage caused by the fight. "That's gonna leave a scar," she said as she gingerly touched a cut on her cheek. Snapping the mirror closed, she walked towards the front gate of her house. "Well let's do this."

In the distance, the wail of sirens came from the direction of the convenience store.

Chapter 9: Homecoming

Walking up the driveway of her house, she could hear the laughter of her parents and the blaring of the television. As usual, they were watching some sort of reality TV show—Bounty Hunters, Cops or Homeless Fights. *Anything to make themselves seem more civilized,* she thought and opened the door.

The smell of cigarettes rolled over her.

"For fuck's sake, close the fucking door," her father said without looking up from the television. "The glare is messing up the picture."

Melissa closed the door silently, and stood in the gloom of the entryway as she looked at her parents who were still oblivious to what was coming.

"About bloody time! Toss me my smokes," her mother called back to her from where she sat in the living room, holding a hand out expectantly.

A wicked smile came across Melle's face as the tentacles rose out of the armour that still protectively covered her body.

"How about I finally give you what you both always wanted?" She stepped fully into the room as her parents turned to face her, their eyes widening with shock as they took in the girl standing in their living room.

Turning to her father, Melle smiled, her teeth a glaring streak of white across a bruised and blood-stained face. "I can be your special girl," she said and stepped forward, the tentacles writhing menacingly.

Her mother screamed and fell back off her chair as a tentacle snapped out to grab her by the ankle, the spikes bit their way into the flesh and coiled tightly. "Oh no, Mum, you are here for this too."

Ian leapt from his chair as his wife's hysterical screams filled the air. His foot slid on a half-eaten sandwich and he landed against the wall heavily and fell to the ground. Turning, he gaped at the tentacled and blood-stained form of his daughter and pressed himself back into the wall as he shook his head in denial. His wife's screams cut through the shock and rolled out of the way of a tentacle that shot towards him. He flung himself sideways, half falling through the doorway and began to scramble to his feet as he tried to get away. Another tentacle flicked forward, knocked him off balance and he fell forward onto the floor, Melle smiled as she heard the pained grunt as he hit the ground. Tentacles shot forward and whipped along his back, cutting deep gouges into the flesh beneath the fabric. The faded blue shirt was slowly turning red as he cried out in pain.

Casually Melle reached for the cheese puffs, as she wrapped a tentacle around her father's foot and pulled him back into the room. Stepping forward, she straddled his bleeding back as the tentacles held him still, ignoring his cries. Daintily, Melle pulled back one of the ripped flaps of skin and fabric, flecks of fatty tissue and membrane covered her long fingers as she methodically stuffed cheese puffs into her father's open wounds. Humming in time with his screams of pain, she giggled as she pushed the edges of the wound together and slowly pressed down until crunched bloody bits of Cheese Puffs started to ooze out.

Standing, she stepped across his prone form and pressed her foot down onto the side of his head, pinning it to the floor. "You are my father," she hissed angrily. "You were meant to protect me." She stomped her foot down with force, feeling satisfaction as something cracked. "You don't try to fuck your daughter, you fat fucking cheese puff." He cried out as her foot came down again, harder this time, the force of the blow snapping his jaw and knocking teeth loose to skitter across the laminated floor. He gurgled and liquid poured out from his mouth as he inhaled sharply, choked on his tongue and vomited. The stench hit Melle's nose and she almost gagged, almost.

Melle didn't know how long she stood there looking down on her broken father, but the sun had set and he had stopped moving.

Blinking dry eyes, Melle turned to regard her mother who had lapsed into quiet sobs, mumbling incoherent words as she held her bleeding ankle, which was still grasped firmly by the tentacle. Noticing the movement, Kellie looked up into the cold eyes of her daughter. "Melle, this is not you. Please stop."

Melle ignored the woman and turned back to her father's body. Tentacles ripped the head free and brought it to her as she turned to face her mother. Smiling, Melle grabbed the dead man's unhinged jaw and made a talking movement while moving it around like a broken bobble-head toy. "Stop? Like how you stopped me from harassing my daughter," she said in the deep, mocking voice of her father. "Oh, Kel, what a card. Now it's your turn to be violated by me and my new pal." She let go of the head and it plopped back down into the mess of vomit and blood on the floor.

The sirens were louder now, most likely they had found Mickey at the park.

"For years, you pushed me around and made me feel like I was worthless. Well not anymore," Melle said with finality.

"Please, baby, no," Kellie begged, but Melle's eyes were cold to her pleas.

We can deal with her and then the police, Glurmo murmured soothingly across her angry mind. *Our bond has grown and power levels are approaching heights I have only ever dreamed of.* To prove a point, Glurmo extended the suit over her whole body, covering Melle in warmth as a green shimmer ran across the surface and power filled her.

Tilting her head, Melle smiled down at her mother. "Time to go, Mum, but let's make this split quick." Sparks of energy shot from the suit and down the tentacles as more sprung out to encase her mother in a writhing mass. The mouths lashed and fed as the lights from the approaching police cars shone through the windows, illuminating the room in red and blues.

Melle extended her arms and watched the exo-suit ripple and flex with her movements. "So, what else can this armour do, Glurmo?" An LED display spread across her vision, highlighting the room in greens and reds as it scanned the surroundings. "Oh wow," Melle murmured, "It's just like that movie about the robot from the future!"

With the power we took from your parents, we now have full systems online which seem to include weapons, Glurmo responded.

"Weapons?" Melle bounced in excitement as two barrels opened on the chest of her suit. "Frickin' gun titties? Heck, Yeah! Let's go try them out and say hello to our visitors!" Rushing to the entryway, she swung open the door, and went outside.

Let's indeed, said Glurmo as they targeted the first police car. *Let's take this pathetic planet over.*

**To Be Continued in the novel
Slug Girl vs The Video Nasties**

Thanks

This book would not be complete without the love and support of Anne Mortleman Chambers, Eloise James, Danielle Shaw, Saber Rain, Serena Worker and Elizabeth Gardner. Naturally I wrote you all as characters in Slug Girl vs The Video Nasties and mostly everything that happens is terrible. Although I am sure some of you may deserve it.